featuring
APPLEJACK

STORY BY **Bobby Curnow**
ART and LYRICS BY **Brenda Hickey**
COLORS BY **Heather Breckel**
LETTERS BY **Neil Uyetake**

ABDOPUBLISHING.COM

Reinforced library bound edition published in 2015 by Spotlight, a division of ABDO, PO Box 398166, Minneapolis, Minnesota 55439. Spotlight produces high-quality reinforced library bound editions for schools and libraries. Published by agreement with IDW.

Printed in the United States of America, North Mankato, Minnesota.
112014
012015

LIBRARY OF CONGRESS CATALOGING-IN-PUBLICATION DATA

Curnow, Bobby.
Applejack / writer, Bobby Curnow ; artist, Brenda Hickey. -- Reinforced library bound edition.
pages cm. -- (My little pony. Pony tales)
Summary: "Applejack prepares the farm for Hearth's Warming Eve when the Sass Squash appears"-- Provided by publisher.
ISBN 978-1-61479-331-1
1. Graphic novels. I. Hickey, Brenda, illustrator. II. Title.
PZ7.7.C88Ap 2015
741.5'973--dc23

2014036761

Spotlight

A Division of ABDO
abdopublishing.com

THAAAT'S THE TICKET, APPLE BLOOM! HOLD 'ER STEADY!

WE KEEP THIS PACE UP, AND WE'LL BE UP TO OUR EYEBALLS IN APPLE SAUCE IN NO TIME!
PONIES SURE DO LOVE OUR APPLE TREATS THIS TIME A YEAR, GRANNY!

WELL, I CAN'T BLAME 'EM! HEARTH'S WARMING EVE IS ALL 'BOUT FOLKS COMIN' TOGETHER!
AND WHEN FOLKS COME TOGETHER, YOU CAN BET YOUR BIPPER THEY'LL WANT SOME TASTY TREATS TO ENJOY.

BUT AS BUSY AS WE MAY GET, WE MUST NEEEVER FORGET THAT IT'S ALSO A TIME TO SPEND WITH THOSE YOU LOVE THE MOST!
YOU BETCHA, GRANNY!
EYUP.

SLAM!
WHAT ARE Y'ALL DOIN' STANDING THERE? WE'VE GOT TONS TO DO!
SORTIN' APPLES, PEELING APPLES, CORIN' APPLES, SMUDGING APPLES, MASHING APPLES, CRATING APPLES, DELIVERIN' APPLES—

SPLASH!
YOU SIMMER DOWN NOW, APPLEJACK! HAVING EVERYTHING JUST SO AIN'T WHAT THIS HOLIDAY IS ABOUT!
I KNOW, GRANNY—BUT THIS SEASON IS IMPORTANT TO THE FARM... AND THE FAMILY!
I COULDN'T BEAR MYSELF IF I KNEW I WASN'T DOIN' ALL I COULD!
AND WE ALL APPRECIATE IT, SIS! BUT YOU DON'T HAVE TO WORK ALL THE TIME, DO YA?
THAT'S RIGHT! TAKE SOME TIME TO ENJOY YERSELF.
EYUP!
DON'T Y'ALL WORRY ABOUT ME. I'M GONNA ENJOY MYSELF AS LONG AS MY FAMILY'S HAPPY. THIS IS GOING TO BE THE BEST HEARTH'S WARMING EVE EVER!

ZZZZZ
SHNORE!
Z
DING!
OOOOOOHH

THE NEXT MORNING.
WHY, I COULD HAVE SLEPT TILL NEXT HEARTH'S WARMING EVE. BUT A FARMER'S WORK WAITS FOR NO PONY!
AIN'T THAT RIGHT, Y'ALL?
Y'ALL?
LOOK
LOOK
APPLE FRITTERS
APPLE FRITTERS
APPLE FRITTERS
APPLE FRITTERS
APPLEJACK! LOOK! IT'S TERRIBLE!
LOTS OF THE APPLES HAVE BEEN STOLEN...
...AND REPLACED WITH SQUASHES!
WHAT IN TARNATION?! HOW COULD THIS HAPPEN? WHO COULDA DONE SUCH A THING?
AIN'T IT OBVIOUS?
IT'S THE SASS SQUASH!

SASS WHAAA?
BOING

C'MON YOUNG 'UNS! I'LL TELL YOU AAALL ABOUT IT.

WAAAY BACK WHEN WE WERE FIRST GETTING THIS FARM OFF THE GROUND, IT SEEMED LIKE THE WORK WOULD NEVER END! WE HAD TO RAISE THE BARN, PLANT THE ORCHARD, DIG THE WELL...
...DAWN TO DUSK, IT WAS WORK, WORK, POLKA, AND WORK!
ALL SO WE COULD HAVE THE FINEST APPLE ORCHARD IN EQUESTRIA!
"YOU COULD IMAGINE OUR SURPRISE WHEN WE AWOKE ONE DAY TO FIND DOZENS OF TREES' APPLES WERE REPLACED WITH *SQUASHES!*
"WHO, OR *WHAT*, WAS BEHIND THIS MYSTERIOUS HAPPENING?
"WELL, HONK MY NOSE AND SHINE MY HOOF, I WAS GOING TO FIND OUT!"

"I STAKED OUT THE AREA FOR WEEKS! I HAD DONE NEAR GIVEN UP HOPE, TILL ONE DAY...
Rustle
Rustle
!

"THAT'S WHEN I SAW IT! NEVER IN ALL MY YEARS THEN OR SINCE HAD I SEEN ANYTHING LIKE IT!"

WHAT WAS IT, GRANNY?
I DON'T NEED TO TELL YOU, I CAN SHOW YOU!
LUCKILY, I HAD MY CAMERA AT THE TIME!

YOU CAN'T TELL FROM THE PHOTO, BUT IT WAS DANCING, RIGHT THERE IN FRONT OF ME!
AND NOT JUST A NORMAL DANCE, HEAVENS NO!
IT WAS A SASSY DANCE!

I MUSTA SPOOKED IT, 'CUZ WE NEVER DID SEE IT, NOR ITS SQUASHES, EVER AGAIN.
TILL NOW, THAT IS!
SLAM!

WELL, IT'S NOT GONNA CAUSE ANY MORE MISCHIEF THIS HOLIDAY!
I'M GONNA CATCH IT!

OH! OH! WE COULD PUT ON A PLAY! THAT IT WOULD WANT TO COME AND WATCH?
OR, OR... I COULD PLAY MY FIDDLE! "MUSIC SOOTHES THE SAVAGE BEAST"!

MAYBE IF WE COATED THE GROUND WITH GUM BALLS IT WOULD TRIP ON 'EM?
WHOOSH
WHOOSH
WE COULD TRAIN WINONA TO SNIFF IT OUT!
MAGNETS! HOW DO THEY WORK?
?
WHOOSH!

I KNOW! I KNOW! LET'S DIG A BIG PIT AND FILL IT WITH QUICKSAND! WE'LL PUT APPLES IN THE MIDDLE FOR BAIT!
APPLE TRAP!
BUMP

NET.

WELL NOW, I BET IF WE ALL PUT OUR HEADS TOGETHER, WE'LL BE ABLE TO FIGURE SOMETHIN' OUT! WORKING TOGETHER IS WHAT HEARTH'S WARMING EVE IS ALL ABOUT, AFTER ALL!

ALSO, I CAN BANG POTS AND PANS TOGETHER! ALL CRITTERS HATE A COMMOTION!

SPLASH!
Y'ALL DON'T FRET. I'LL CATCH IT. I WANT Y'ALL TO ENJOY THE HOLIDAY.
I'M NOT GONNA LET EVERYTHING BE RUINED BY A NO GOOD VARMINT!
Flap
BUT APPLEJACK! YOU CAN'T DO IT ALL BY YOURSELF! ISN'T THAT RIGHT, BIG MAC?
EYUP.
THEY'RE RIGHT! WE HAVE TO DO THIS TOGETHER!
NOW, I WON'T HEAR OF IT. THIS HOLIDAY MEANS TOO MUCH. YOU THREE CONTINUE THE HEARTH'S WARMING EVE PREPARATIONS, AND BEFORE YOU KNOW IT, I'LL BAG US A SASS SQUASH!

THIS WILL BE A SNAP! THERE AIN'T A PROBLEM IN EQUESTRIA THAT CAN'T BE SOLVED WITH A LITTLE DETERMINATION AND ELBOW GREASE.
BAM!
SMAK!
POW!

JUMP
&
LAND!
THERE WE GO! FIT TO CAGE A BEAR! THREE BEARS, EVEN, I RECKON!
THROW IN A BUSHEL OF OUR MOST IRRESISTIBLE APPLES AS BAIT, AND THINGS ARE ABOUT TO TURN UP APPLEJACK!

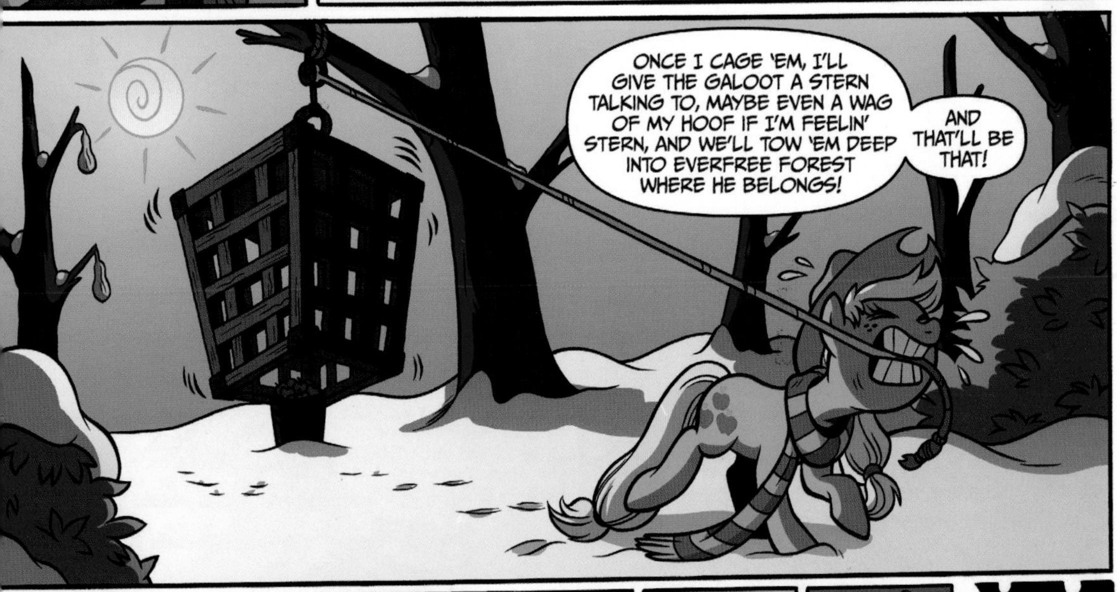
ONCE I CAGE 'EM, I'LL GIVE THE GALOOT A STERN TALKING TO, MAYBE EVEN A WAG OF MY HOOF IF I'M FEELIN' STERN, AND WE'LL TOW 'EM DEEP INTO EVERFREE FOREST WHERE HE BELONGS!
AND THAT'LL BE THAT!

AND NOW TO LET SWEET PATIENCE PLAY IT'S PRECIOUS MELODY.
RUSTL
POP!
IT'S LIKE THE PONY SAYS, "WAITIN' IS THE HARDEST PART"!
APPLE COBBLER. APPLE BURRITO. APPLE... APPLE.
Z

APPLEJACK! WAKE UP!
SNORT CAT BAGELS!
WHA-HUH?
APPLEJACK, YOU FELL ASLEEP!
WELL, MAYBE I JUST RESTED MY EYES FOR A MOMENT, BUT I—
WHAT ARE YOU DOING INSIDE THAT CAGE?
WHAT IN THE WORLD ARE YOU TALKING ABOUT APPLE BLOOM? I'M ON THE...
Dust
...OUTSIDE.

DAG NAB IT! I'VE BEEN BAMBOOZLED!
ARE YOU SURE YOU COULDN'T USE SOME HELP?

NO WAY, NUH-UH, NEGATORY, LITTLE MISSY! I PROMISED Y'ALL THAT I WOULD CAPTURE THIS SASS SQUASH, AND THAT'S EXACTLY WHAT I'M GONNA DO!
AND I DON'T NEED A LICK OF HELP!

...THAT IS, RIGHT AFTER YOU HELP ME OUTTA THIS CAGE.

I'M GOIN' ABOUT THIS TOO REASONABLE-LIKE. TO CAPTURE A SASS SQUASH, I HAVE TO THINK LIKE A SASS SQUASH.
"GORG! I LOVE THE WOODS."
"HURK! BEIN' ELUSIVE IS THE LIFE FOR ME!"
BORK!
"MOSS IS COMFORTABLE AND DELICIOUS!"
NOW I'M GETTIN' IT!
....
WHAT THE HECK ARE Y'ALL LOOKIN' AT?
WAIT A HOOF-STOMPIN' MINUTE! THAT'S IT!
I GOTTA LOOK TO SEE.
ZOOOOOOOOO
MMOOOO
WELP, SHE'S LOST IT.
NOD

WHEW! THAT'S THE LAST ONE!
ALL THESE MIRRORS BOUNCE BACK HERE.
IF THAT OVER-RIPE VEGETABLE COMES ANYWHERE *NEAR* THE ORCHARD, I'M SURE TO SEE IT!
AH!
BIG MCINTOSH! STOP CHECKIN' YOURSELF OUT! THESE ARE STRICTLY NON-VANITY MIRRORS!

LET ME GUESS, YOU WANT TO HELP? USING YOUR NET?
EEYUP AND EEYUP.

IF I SAID IT ONCE, I SAID IT AGAIN: I'M GONNA BAG THIS MONSTER ON MY LONESOME.
I APPRECIATE THE CONCERN, BUT YOU AND THE FAMILY SHOULD BE BUSY MAKING SURE EVERYTHING IS READY FOR THE HOLIDAY.
I CAN DO THIS BY MYSELF, AND I'M ABOUT TO PROVE IT.

DOUBLE DANG BLAST IT...!
MIRRORS ALL GONE.
I CAN SEE THAT!

APPLEJACK! APPLEJACK, WHERE ARE YOU? I'VE COME TO TALK SOME SENSE INTO YA!
WHERE COULD THAT FILLY BE?

GRANNY! DON'T MOVE A MUSCLE!
WHA?
BLINK

I'VE GOT THIS PLACE BOOBY-TRAPPED! THIS ENTIRE AREA IS RIGGED WITH TRIP WIRES AND SNARES!
REEL
OH MY!

I'M A WORRIED ABOUT YOU, APPLEJACK.
I KNOW WHAT IT'S LIKE TO GET CAUGHT UP IN THE HUNT FOR THE SASS SQUASH. BUT AT THE END OF THE DAY, THAT CREATURE AIN'T GONNA BE CAUGHT IF IT'S NOT OF A MIND TO.
I DON'T WANT YOU TO LOSE SIGHT OF WHAT'S IMPORTANT HERE. IT'S NOT YOUR JOB TO MAKE EVERYTHING PERFECT!

AW, GRANNY, I APPRECIATE ALL OF THAT, BUT—

WHOAH!
SPROING

...I'VE GOT EVERYTHING UNDER CONTROL.
PLOP!

YOU'LL NEVER BELIEVE!
THIS HEARTH'S WARMING EVE
AN UNWANTED GUEST
BECAME SUCH A PEST
BUT ALL ON MY OWN
I'LL DO IT ALONE
THE TRAPS ARE ALL SET
I WON'T GIVE UP YET!
FREE
THE PLANS ARE IN PLACE
LET'S END THIS RAT RACE!
BUT SOMETHING FEELS WRONG
IT'S TAKING TOO LONG!
XTRA STICKY MOLASSES
TOSS

♪ ♫ BUT HOW COULD THIS BE?! ♩
HE'S OUTSMARTED ME!
THE SCARECROWS HAVE FAILED
AND THE SQUASH HAS BAILED!
♫
♫ ♩ I FEEL LIKE A FOOL
IT'S GETTING TOO CRUEL! ♫
THAT PAINT SHOULD HAVE WORKED
I'M GETTING QUITE IRKED! ♪
THANX
POW
SPLAT!
♫ OH IT'S SUCH A PAIN! ♪
IS IT ALL IN VAIN?
THAT SQUASH HAS ME BEAT
I CAN'T TAKE DEFEAT!
♫ ♪ ♫

Tropica Get Away For Squash!
GRRR...

DAG NAB IT!

NOTHIN' WORKS! I'VE TRIED EVERYTHING! IT'S ALWAYS ONE STEP AHEAD A' ME!
DARN! DANG! SHOOT!
FIDDLESTICKS AND MARMALADE!

Huff
Huff

"IT'S NOT YOUR JOB TO MAKE EVERYTHING PERFECT."

THEN WHOSE JOB IS IT, GRANNY?

...AND THAT'S WHERE THE PHRASE "NEVER TRUST AN ONION" COMES FROM!
SIP
UM.. EXCUSE ME, Y'ALL.
I'M SORRY, I... I COULDN'T CAPTURE THE SASS SQUASH. IT'S JUST TOO DANG ELUSIVE.
I... I'VE FAILED YA.
NOW, NOW APPLEJACK. DON'T BE HARD ON YOURSELF. THAT SQUASH HAS ELUDED CAPTURE FOR GENERATIONS.
I KNOW. IT'S JUST... I WANTED TO CATCH IT SO Y'ALL COULD ENJOY THE HOLIDAYS IN PEACE.
HEARTH'S WARMING EVE IS TOMORROW. WHO KNOWS WHAT IT WILL DO TO OUR REMAINING SUPPLIES OVERNIGHT?
NONE OF THAT'S IMPORTANT NOW, DEARIE. WHAT'S IMPORTANT IS THAT WE'RE A FAMILY, AND WE'RE TOGETHER.
YOU'RE ABSOLUTELY RIGHT, GRANNY! I'VE BEEN GOIN' ABOUT THIS ALL PIG-HEADED. THIS HOLIDAY'S NOT ABOUT DOIN' THINGS BY YOURSELF!
IT'S ABOUT COMIN' TOGETHER, AND WORKING WITH THOSE YOU LOVE MOST!
AND BY GOLLY, THAT'S JUST WHAT WE'LL DO! WE'LL WORK *TOGETHER* AND CATCH THIS CRITTER!
OH BOY! THIS'LL BE *FUN!*

OKAY, THAT'S A WRAP! LET'S HUDDLE UP!
EVERYONE KNOW WHAT THEY'RE SUPPOSED TO DO?
YEAH!
EYUP.
YOU GOT IT, MISSY!
THEN LET'S SHOW THIS VARMINT IT'S MESSIN' WITH THE WRONG FAMILY!
APPLE FAMILY...
GO!
YOU'RE UP, GRANNY!
BANG! BANG
HOOT HOOT! I'M COMIN' TO GETCHA, YOU GREAT GREEN GOOFUS!
BANG
BANG
BE READY, APPLE BLOOM. YOU NEVER KNOW WHEN—

CRRAASH!
GRAH!
GURH?
GRAAHH!
GURH GRAH?!
NET SOUND
WE GOT 'EM! WE GOT 'EM! WE—
HUH? WHAT'S IT DOIN'?

HA HA! I GOT YOU YOUNG 'UNS GOOD!
WHAT IN THE HAY NOW?!
??
??

Y'SEE, AFTER I RAN INTO THE FOREST I SUITED UP INTO THIS OLD COSTUME I MADE YEARS AGO.
Y'SEE?
BUT... WHY WOULD YOU DO ALL OF THIS, GRANNY?

TO BRING US ALL TOGETHER, OF COURSE! WE WERE SO BUSY PREPARING FOR THE HOLIDAY THAT WE FORGOT TO SPEND TIME WITH EACH OTHER.
SAME THING HAPPENED BACK WHEN I WAS A LITTLE GIRL, AND THE FARM WAS JUST GETTIN' STARTED. THE IDEA OF HUNTIN' A SASS SQUASH GOT OUR MIND OFF OUR WORK, AND LET US SPEND SOME QUALITY TIME TOGETHER!
I THOUGHT IT MIGHT BE TIME FER A REPEAT PERFORMANCE!

UNTIL APPLEJACK TOOK ALL THE RESPONSIBILITY FOR HERSELF, LIKE SHE ALWAYS DOES!
EVEN THOUGH A FAMILY SHOULD SHARE WORK AND PLAY TOGETHER!
LUCKILY, YOU EVENTUALLY REALIZED THAT ALL BY YERSELF, APPLEJACK. JUST LIKE I KNEW YE WOULD!
POKE!

SHUCKS, YOU'RE RIGHT, GRANNY. I *DID* GET A LITTLE CARRIED AWAY.
LUCKILY, I'VE GOT Y'ALL TO KEEP ME ON TRACK.

THAT'S RIGHT! 'CUZ WE'RE A FAMILY!
EEEEYUP!
DARN TOOTIN'!

"DEAR PRINCESS CELESTIA,
"IF THERE'S ONE THING I'VE LEARNED THIS HEARTH'S WARMING EVE, IT'S THAT HOLIDAYS CAN GET A MIGHT CRAZY. SEEMS LIKE THERE'S ALWAYS A MILLION THINGS TO DO, AND SO LITTLE TIME TO DO IT!
APPLE FRITTERS
APPLE FRITTERS
"BUT IF YOU DON'T TAKE A MOMENT TO SLOW DOWN—REALLY SLOW DOWN—AND SPEND A LITTLE TIME WITH YOUR FAMILY, YOU MIGHT MISS WHAT THE HOLIDAY IS TRULY ALL ABOUT...

"...COMIN' TOGETHER, AND APPRECIATING JUST HOW IMPORTANT EVERY SINGLE PONY IS. AFTER ALL, EVEN THOSE CLOSEST TO YOU..."
Z

IT COULDN'T BE...

"...MIGHT JUST SURPRISE YA.
"SINCERELY, APPLEJACK."

YOU ENJOY NOW, BIG FELLER. YER WORK'S ALL DONE.

OH, AND HAPPY HEARTH'S WARMING EVE TO YA!

THE END